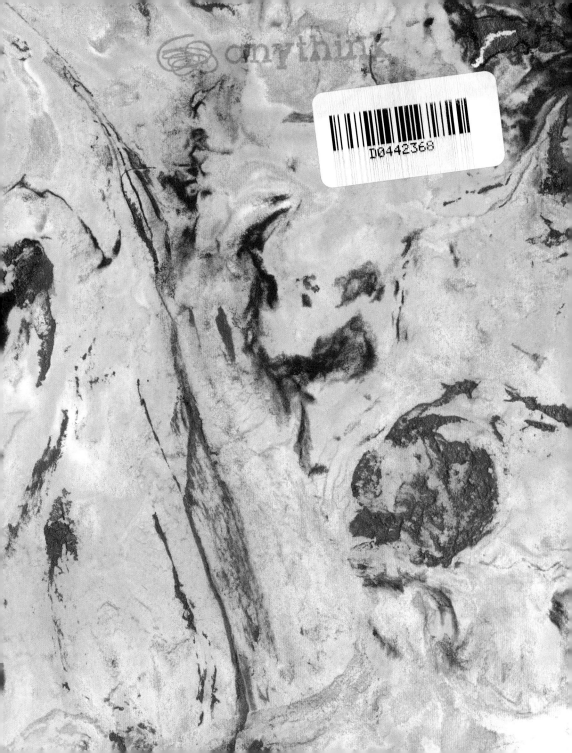

This edition first published in 2020 by Gecko Press
PO Box 9335, Wellington 6141, New Zealand
info@geckopress.com

English-language edition © Gecko Press Ltd 2020
Translation © Julia Marshall 2020

Original title: *Förvandlingen* © Anna Höglund, Stockholm 2018
English edition published in agreement with Koja Agency

The cost of this translation was defrayed by a subsidy
from the Swedish Arts Council, gratefully acknowledged.

Illustrations made with copper plate etching and watercolors.

Edited by Penelope Todd
Typesetting by Spencer Levine
Printed in China by Everbest Printing Co. Ltd,
an accredited ISO 14001 & FSC-certified printer

ISBN hardback: 978-1-776572-73-1

For more curiously good books, visit geckopress.com

Anna Höglund

THE STONE GIANT

GECKO PRESS

There was once a child who lived on an island in the sea with her father who was a knight.

One morning her father said, "My dear child, there's a very dangerous giant out there who is turning people to stone. I must go and fight it. You'll have to stay and look after yourself for a while."

And so he jumped into his boat with all his swords and muskets, and rowed away.

The child was alone. That day she fixed everything in the house that was broken and she watched the sea.

But no boat appeared.

When evening came
she said goodnight
to herself in the mirror.
What would happen,
she wondered, if the giant
looked in a mirror?

The child kept a candle
burning in the window
so her father could find his
way home.

For many days and nights
she waited.

He should have been
back a long time ago,
thought the child.

One evening the candle
burned right down
and went out.
It was terribly dark.

The child took her mirror
and a knife and went down
to the beach.

The water was as black
and shiny as oil.

I can't see a thing and
I don't know how this will
turn out, thought the child.
If only I had a boat.

She swam straight out into the dark. There was no sign of land in any direction. But the child could swim and the water carried her.

The island was soon far behind and the darkness enveloped her. She didn't know how long she had been swimming when her feet finally touched the bottom.

The sun came up and dried her clothes.
A new land lay before her.

A gleaming path led into the forest.
The child decided to follow it.

All day she followed

the path.

When night fell she could no longer see where she was going. Then a light appeared up ahead. It shone in the window of a little house and the child went and knocked at the door.

"Come in," called the old woman. "Where are you going?"

"To save my father from the giant who's turning people to stone."

"Then you need to be well prepared, little friend," said the woman. "Stay here for the night. You must eat and rest."

The next morning she gave the child one of her umbrellas to protect her from the giant's dangerous eyes.

"Because it's the giant's gaze that turns all living things to stone," the old woman explained.

"That's what I thought," said the child. "Thank you very much."

Soon the child came
to the barren country
where the giant lived.
Everything was dead
and faded and very quiet.
No flowers grew there,
and no birds sang.

She had not gone far before
the ground began to shake.
The giant was coming
closer. The child snapped
open her umbrella.

"Who is under that peculiar roof? Come out so I can see you," said the giant, scraping her long nails over the umbrella.

"I'm shy," said the child, "but I can make a hole in the roof for you to peep through."

The giant gave a nasty laugh. But the child took her knife and cut a hole in the top of the umbrella…

…and quickly set her mirror into the opening.

The giant stared in. She met her own gaze in the mirror. Her eyes grew wide as the magic began to work against her. She was turning back into stone.

The child looked around. The barren landscape was coming to life. The rocks and boulders were people again. And look, there was the child's father, alive and well.

From that day on there was peace in the land, and the child was never again alone.

With thanks to Elsa Beskow
who inspired this book with her
unforgettable story *Tripp, Trapp,
Trull och j'tten Dum-dum*.